P9-BJJ-309

A NOTE TO PARENTS

When your children are ready to "step into reading," giving them the right books is as crucial to their development as giving them the right food to eat. **Step into Reading**® books feature exciting stories and information reinforced with lively, colorful illustrations that make learning to read fun, satisfying, and rewarding. We have even taken *extra* steps to keep your child engaged by offering Step into Reading Sticker books, Step into Reading Math books, and Step into Reading Phonics books, in addition to fabulous fiction and nonfiction.

Learning to read, Step by Step:

- **Super Early** books (Preschool–Kindergarten) support pre-reading skills. Parent and child can engage in "see and say" reading using the strong picture cues and the few simple words on each page.
- **Early** books (Preschool–Kindergarten) let emergent readers tackle one or two short sentences of large type per page.
- **Step 1** books (Preschool–Grade 1) have the same easy-to-read type as Early, but with more words per page.
- **Step 2** books (Grades 1–3) offer longer and slightly more difficult text while introducing contractions and clauses. Children are often drawn to our exciting natural science nonfiction titles at this level.
- **Step 3** books (Grades 2–3) present paragraphs, chapters, and fully developed plot lines in fiction and nonfiction.
- **Step 4** books (Grades 2–4) feature thrilling nonfiction illustrated with exciting photographs for independent as well as reluctant readers.

Remember: The grade levels assigned to the six steps are intended only as guides. Some children move through all six steps rapidly; others climb the steps over a period of a few years. Either way, these books will help children "step into reading" for life!

To my buddy Christopher Winskill
—J. W.

Copyright © 2003 Disney Enterprises, Inc. All rights reserved under International and
Pan-American Copyright Conventions. Published in the United States by Random House
Children's Books, a division of Random House, Inc., New York, and simultaneously in Canada
by Random House of Canada Limited, Toronto, in conjunction with Disney Enterprises, Inc.
RANDOM HOUSE and colophon are registered trademarks of Random House, Inc. Based on the
Mowgli stories in *The Jungle Book* and *The Second Jungle Book* by Rudyard Kipling.

www.randomhouse.com/kids/disney

Library of Congress Cataloging-in-Publication Data
Winskill, John.
Jungle friends / written by John Winskill.
    p. cm. — (Step into reading. An early book)
Summary: Easy-to-read text introduces a number of Mowgli's friends from
the animated Disney version of *The Jungle Book*.
 ISBN 0-7364-2089-4 —ISBN 0-7364-8017-X (alk. paper)
[1. Jungle animals—Fiction.] I. Jungle book (Motion picture) II.Title. III. Series.
PZ7.W729897 Ju 2003
[E]—dc21
2002004538
Printed in the United States of America   10 9 8 7 6 5 4 3 2 1

STEP INTO READING, RANDOM HOUSE, and the Random House colophon are registered trademarks
of Random House, Inc.

Step into Reading®

Walt Disney's THE JUNGLE Book

Jungle Friends

An Early Book

By John Winskill

Illustrated by the Disney Global Artists

Random House New York

Mowgli lives in
the jungle.

He has lots of friends.

Furry friends.

Scaly friends.

Feathered friends.

Giant friends.

Mowgli has fun with
his jungle friends.

Every day they
march and play.

They run.

They swing.

They eat.

They dance.

But of all his
jungle friends . . .

Big Baloo is his favorite.

Baloo loves his
"Little Buddy."

And Mowgli loves Baloo.